# The sailor and the sea witch

by Preston McClear

illustrations by Nicholas Dollak

To Mrs. LoCasio,
Keep Sailing Through
Books!
— Preston McClear

FIRST PRINTING



Published in the United States of America by Malibu Books For Children,
a division of Malibu Films, Inc.

48 Broad Street #134
Red Bank, N.J. 07701
Website: http://www.MalibuBooks.com
email: MalibuInc@aol.com



Printed in Hong Kong

10 9 8 7 6 5 4 3 2

ISBN 1-929084-11-0

LCCN

Jacket and book design by Nicholas Dollak

*This book is dedicated to my niece*
*Courtney,*
*and to my favorite actress*
*Michelle Yeoh.*

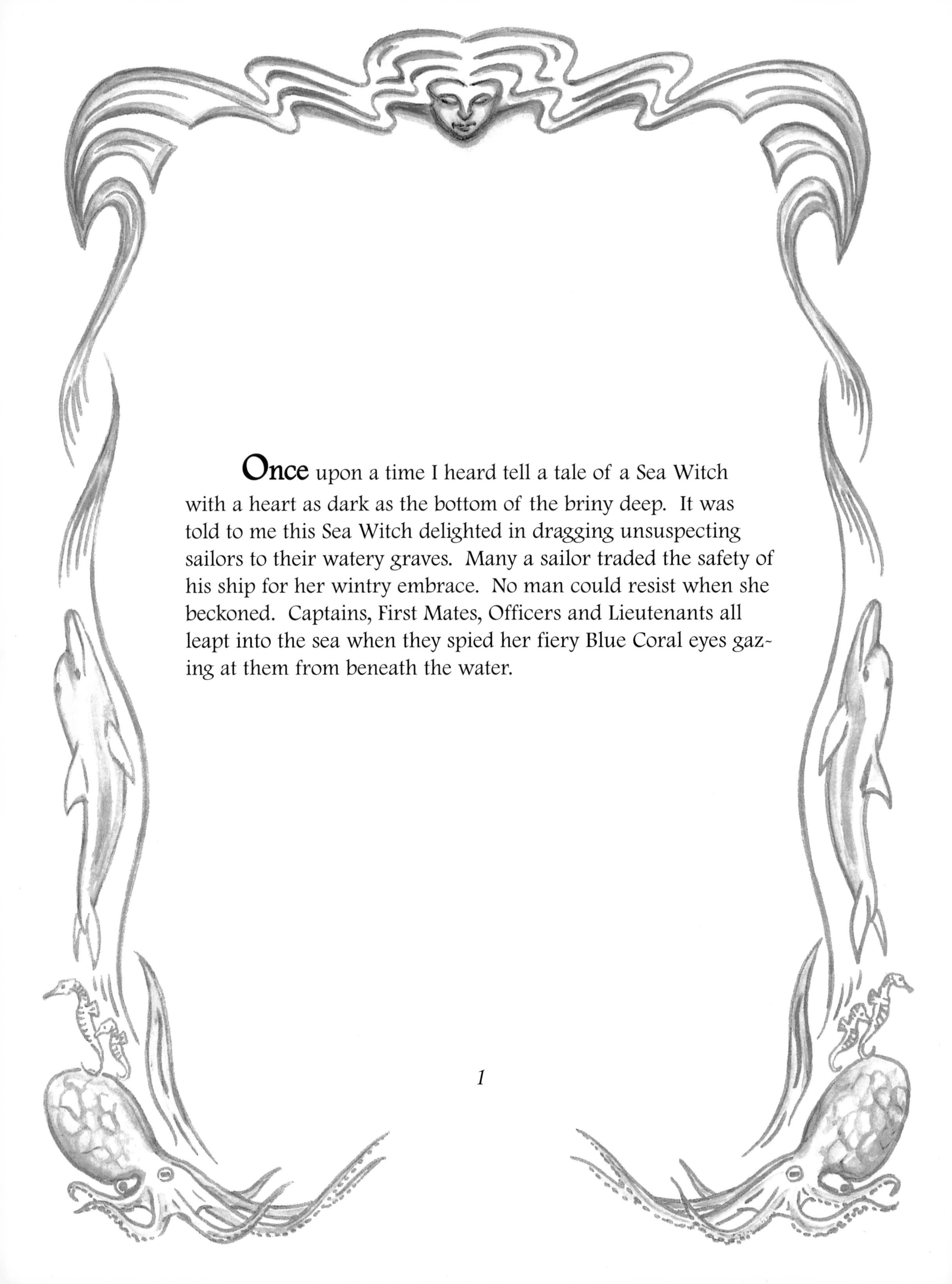

**Once** upon a time I heard tell a tale of a Sea Witch with a heart as dark as the bottom of the briny deep. It was told to me this Sea Witch delighted in dragging unsuspecting sailors to their watery graves. Many a sailor traded the safety of his ship for her wintry embrace. No man could resist when she beckoned. Captains, First Mates, Officers and Lieutenants all leapt into the sea when they spied her fiery Blue Coral eyes gazing at them from beneath the water.

©1998 N. Dollak

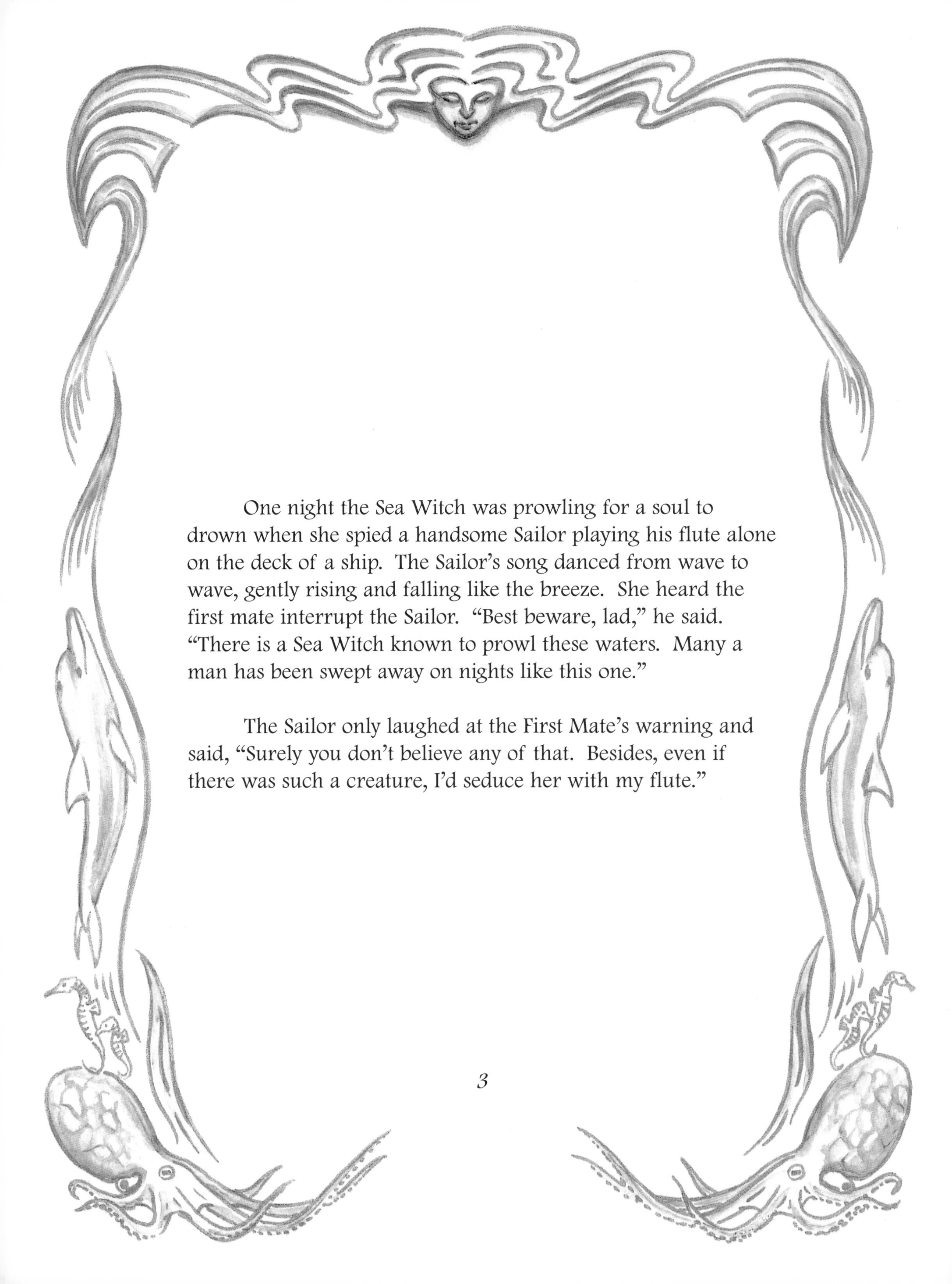

One night the Sea Witch was prowling for a soul to drown when she spied a handsome Sailor playing his flute alone on the deck of a ship. The Sailor's song danced from wave to wave, gently rising and falling like the breeze. She heard the first mate interrupt the Sailor. "Best beware, lad," he said. "There is a Sea Witch known to prowl these waters. Many a man has been swept away on nights like this one."

The Sailor only laughed at the First Mate's warning and said, "Surely you don't believe any of that. Besides, even if there was such a creature, I'd seduce her with my flute."

©1998 N. Dollak

The Sea Witch became angry when she heard the Sailor laughing. Such insolence from a man was more than she could bear. What was he to her? The thought of drowning him delighted her.

As the Sea Witch reached her treacherous fingers over the deck, the Sailor began to play his flute once more. The Witch was enchanted and couldn't bring herself to drown the Sailor. She let the handsome mariner and his beautiful melody drift on across the sea.

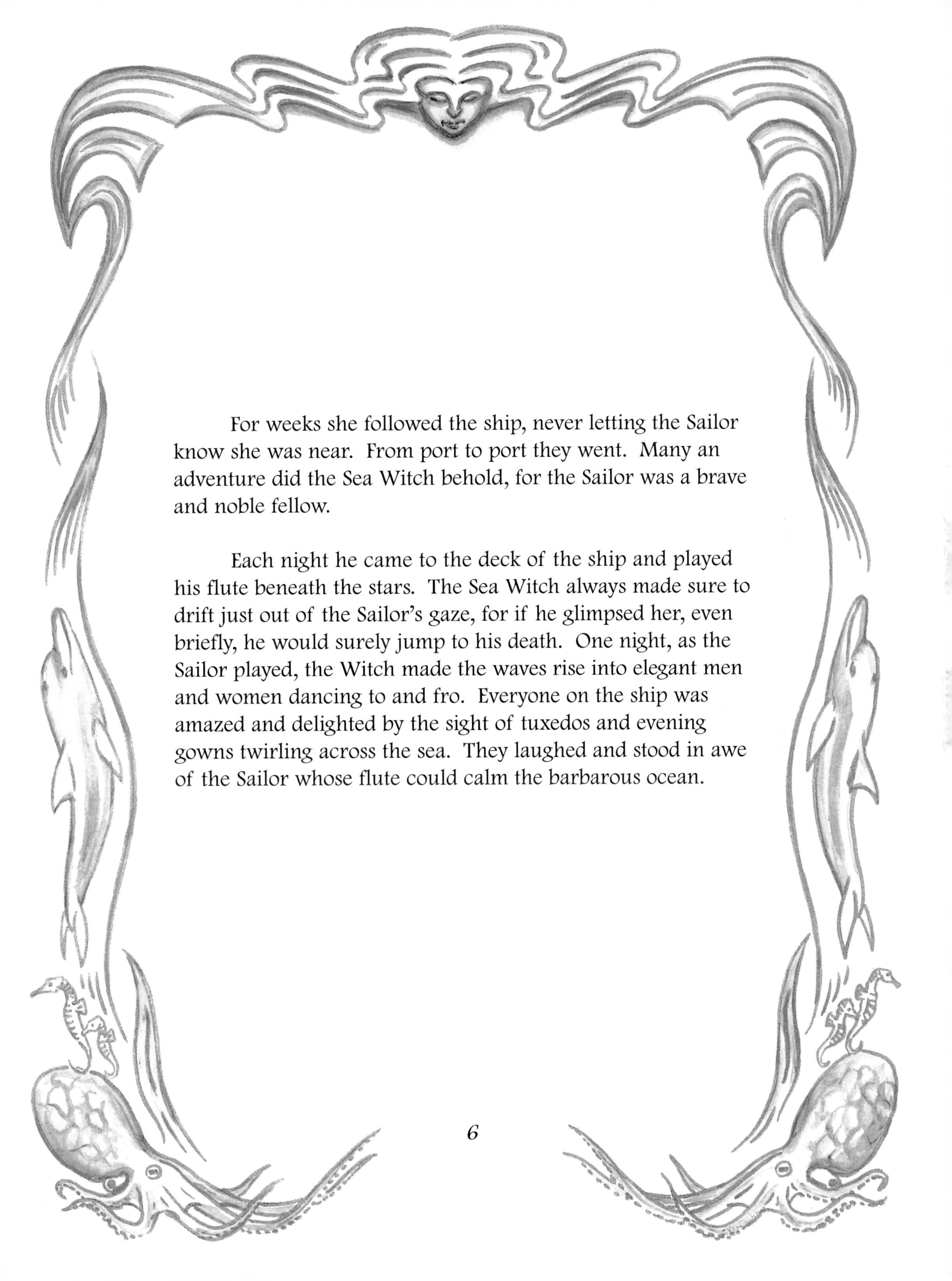

For weeks she followed the ship, never letting the Sailor know she was near. From port to port they went. Many an adventure did the Sea Witch behold, for the Sailor was a brave and noble fellow.

Each night he came to the deck of the ship and played his flute beneath the stars. The Sea Witch always made sure to drift just out of the Sailor's gaze, for if he glimpsed her, even briefly, he would surely jump to his death. One night, as the Sailor played, the Witch made the waves rise into elegant men and women dancing to and fro. Everyone on the ship was amazed and delighted by the sight of tuxedos and evening gowns twirling across the sea. They laughed and stood in awe of the Sailor whose flute could calm the barbarous ocean.

©1998 N. Dollak

On another night, while the Sailor played, the flute slipped from his hand into the water. The Sea Witch disguised herself as a dolphin and snatched the flute back for him. As she rose towards the Sailor with the flute in her beak, their eyes met. Before taking the flute, the Sailor placed his hand upon her brow and smiled. At that moment the Sea Witch fell madly in love with the Sailor.

From his watch the first mate shouted, “Now you’ve done it. You’ve gone to soothing the savage beast. What will become of us?”

Once again the Sailor laughed and said, "I've never seen a beast with eyes like hers. Surely she couldn't be a beast." To the dolphin he added, "After all, you did bring me my flute, didn't you? Thank you, Bright Eyes."

From then on, whenever the Sailor played, the Sea Witch came disguised as a dolphin and danced for him. She swam

alongside the ship day and night, never straying from the Sailor's side. As the months went by she noticed a sadness gathering about the Sailor's song.

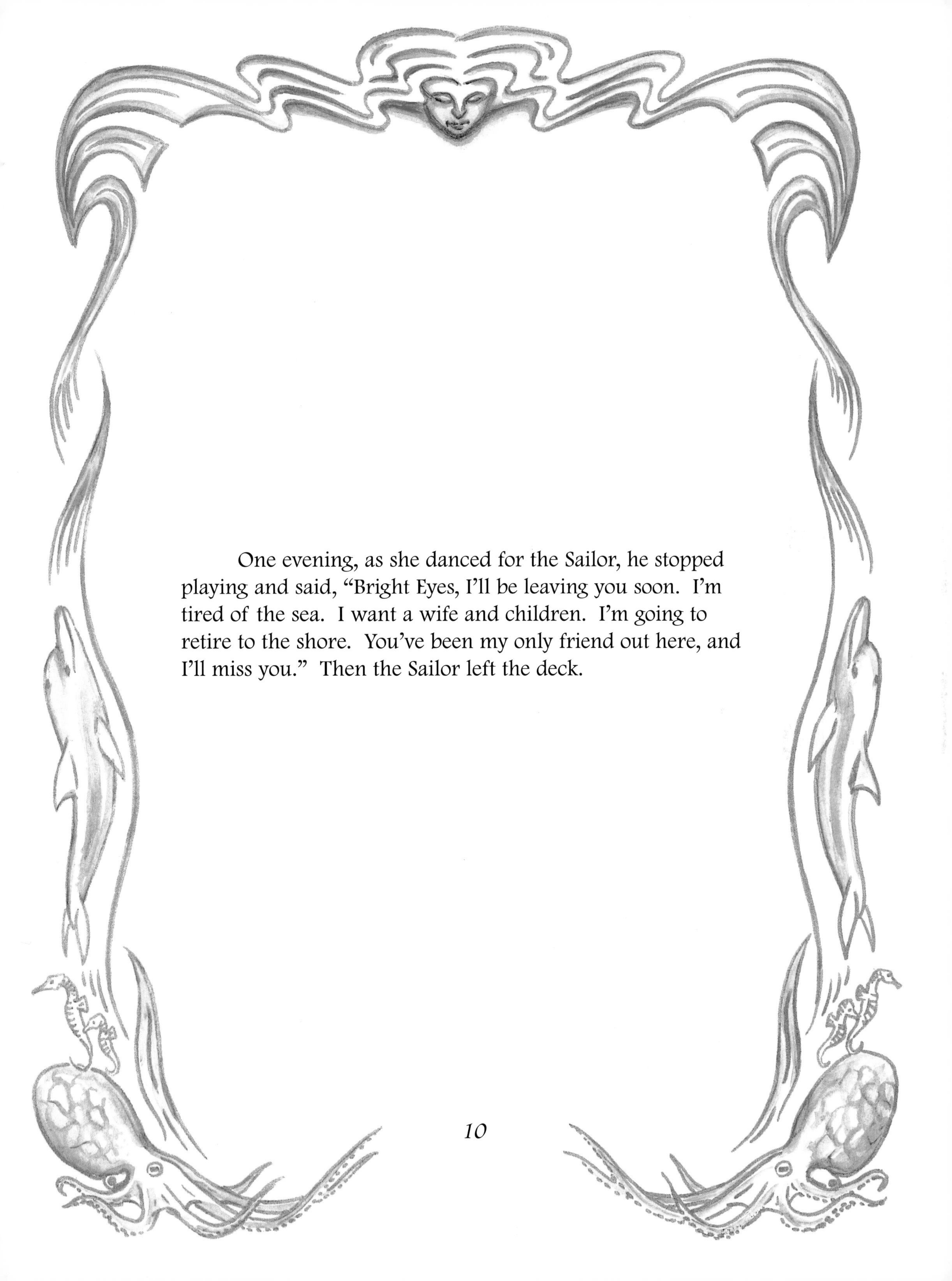

One evening, as she danced for the Sailor, he stopped playing and said, “Bright Eyes, I’ll be leaving you soon. I’m tired of the sea. I want a wife and children. I’m going to retire to the shore. You’ve been my only friend out here, and I’ll miss you.” Then the Sailor left the deck.

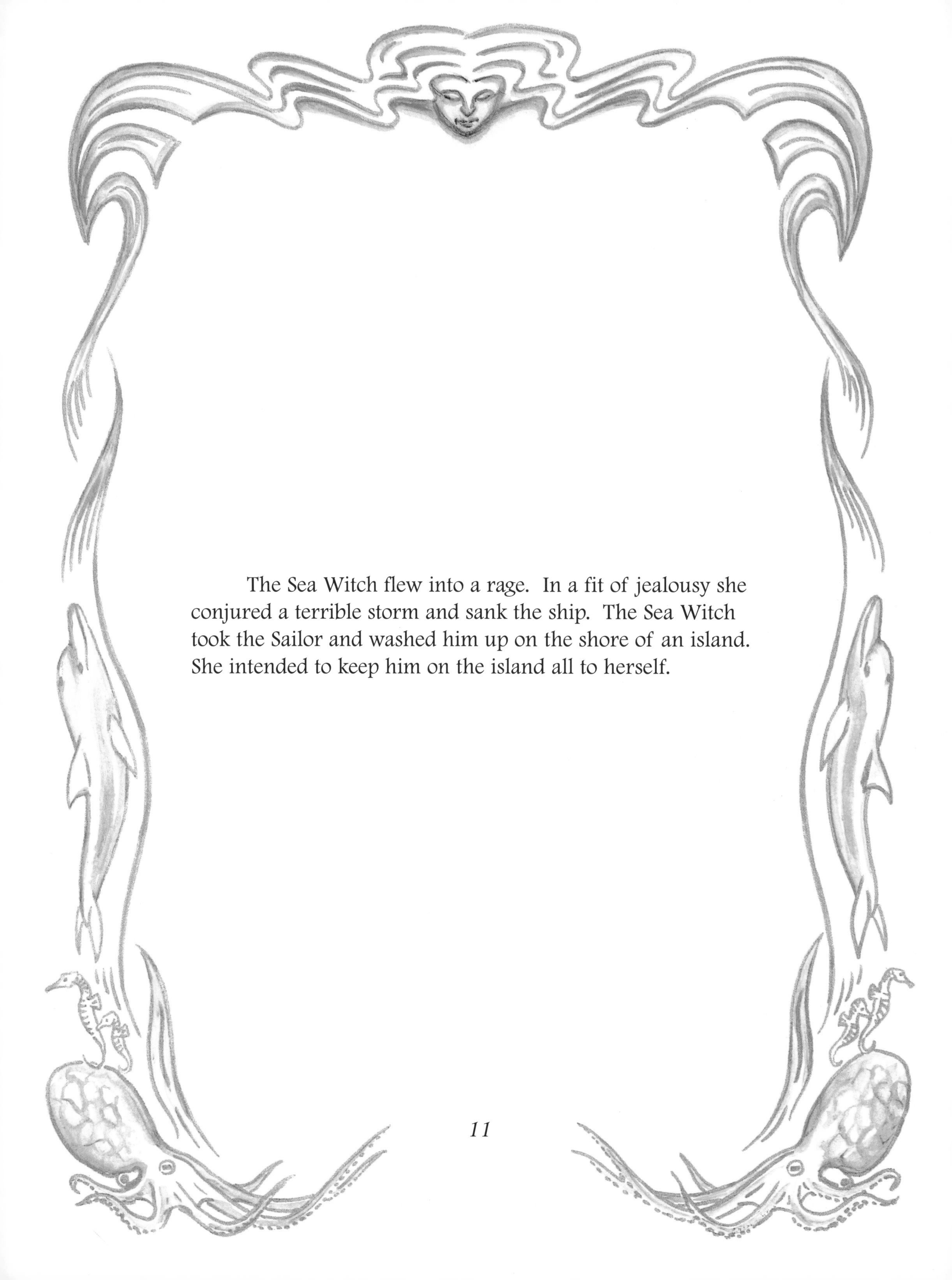

The Sea Witch flew into a rage. In a fit of jealousy she conjured a terrible storm and sank the ship. The Sea Witch took the Sailor and washed him up on the shore of an island. She intended to keep him on the island all to herself.

©1998 N. Dollak

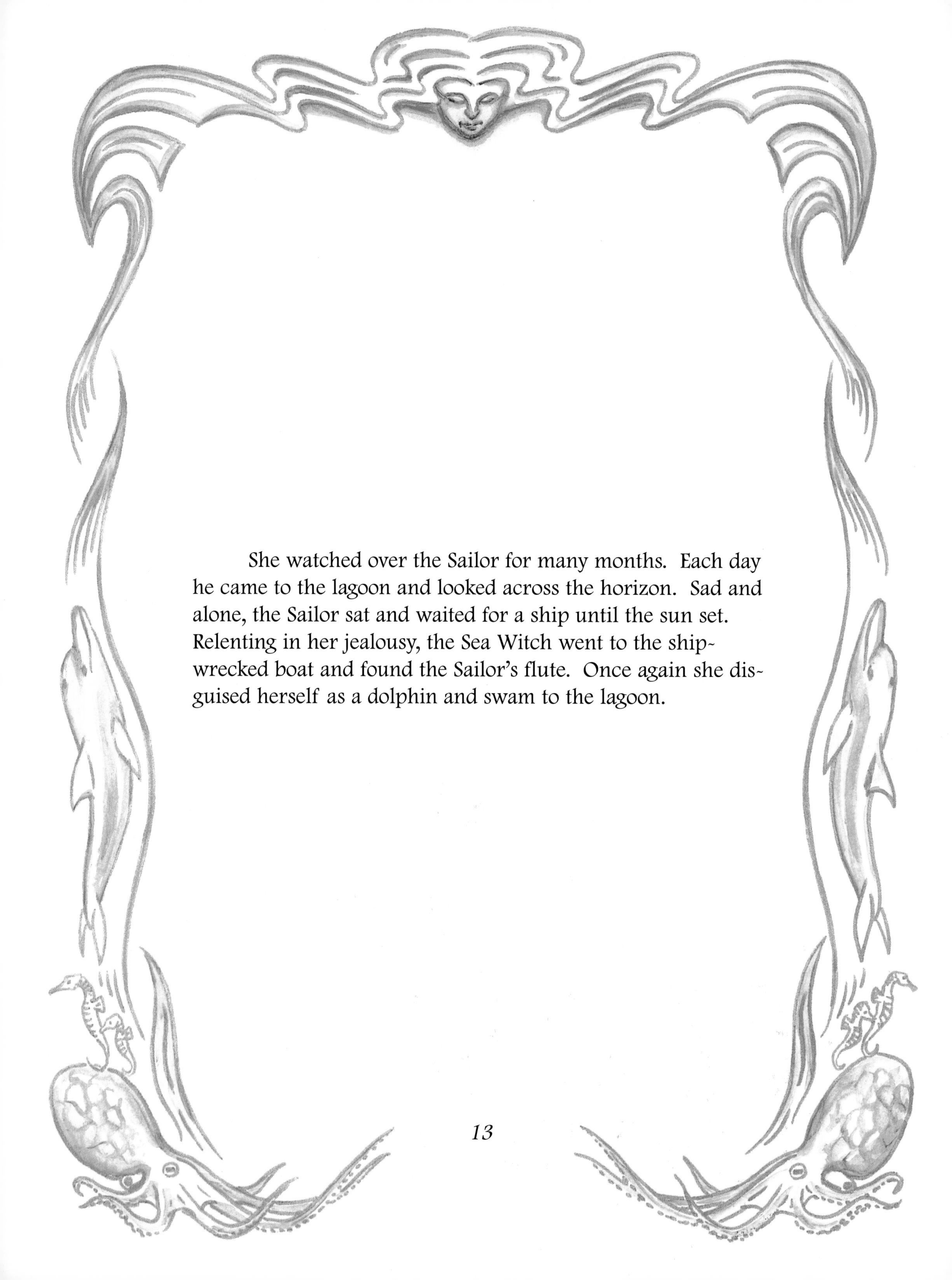

She watched over the Sailor for many months. Each day he came to the lagoon and looked across the horizon. Sad and alone, the Sailor sat and waited for a ship until the sun set. Relenting in her jealousy, the Sea Witch went to the ship-wrecked boat and found the Sailor's flute. Once again she disguised herself as a dolphin and swam to the lagoon.

©2001 N. Dollak

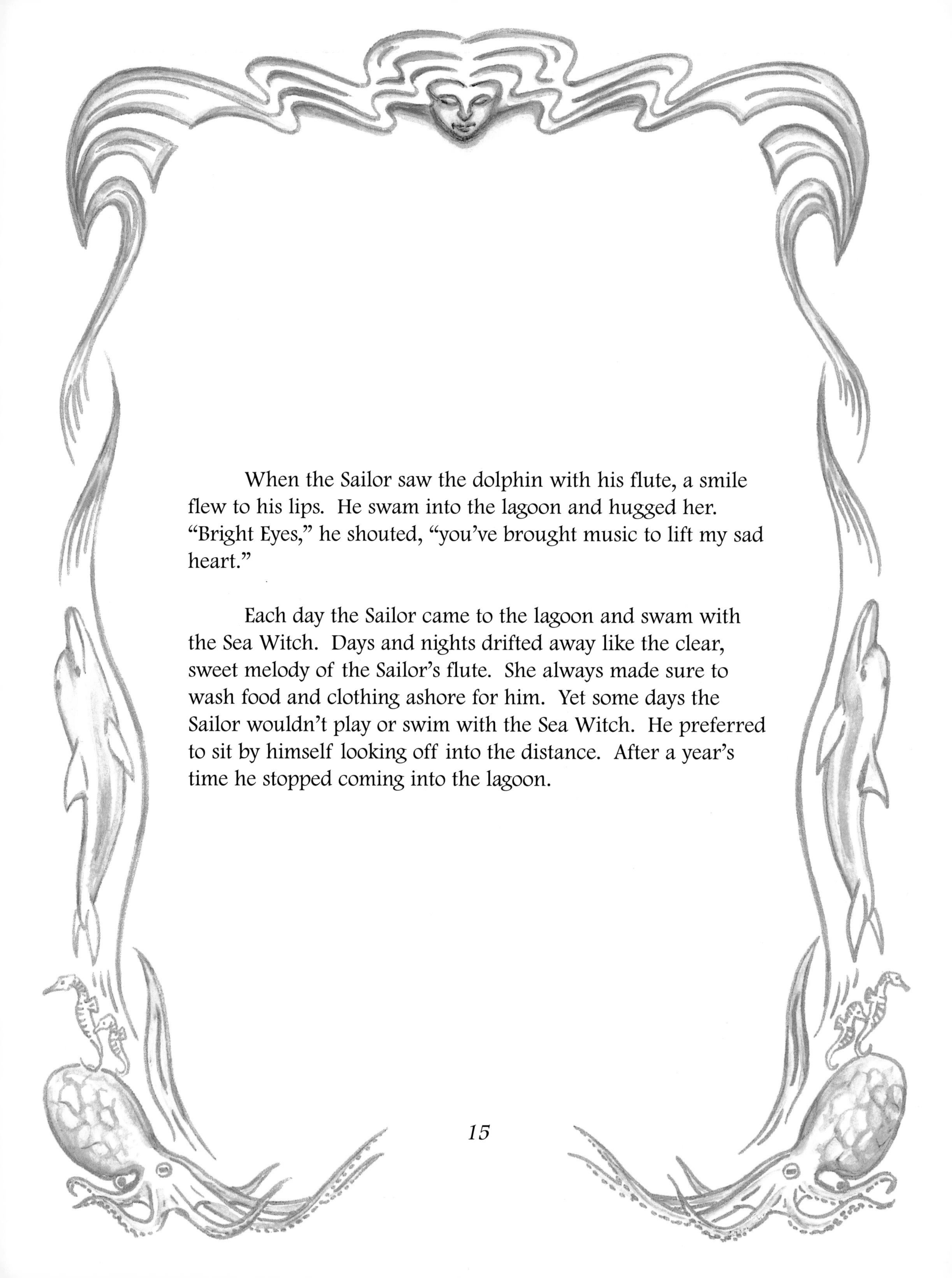

When the Sailor saw the dolphin with his flute, a smile flew to his lips. He swam into the lagoon and hugged her. “Bright Eyes,” he shouted, “you’ve brought music to lift my sad heart.”

Each day the Sailor came to the lagoon and swam with the Sea Witch. Days and nights drifted away like the clear, sweet melody of the Sailor’s flute. She always made sure to wash food and clothing ashore for him. Yet some days the Sailor wouldn’t play or swim with the Sea Witch. He preferred to sit by himself looking off into the distance. After a year’s time he stopped coming into the lagoon.

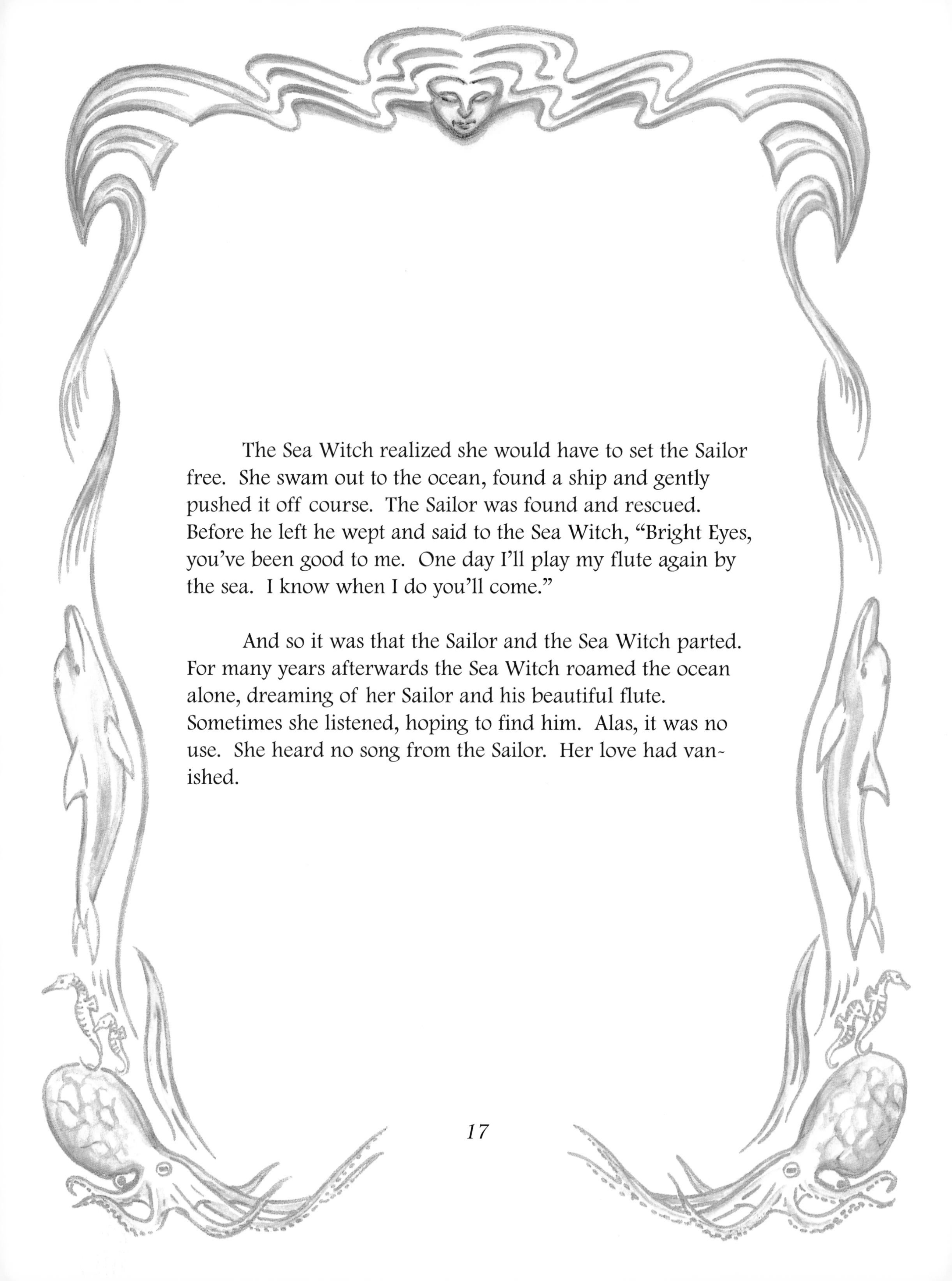

The Sea Witch realized she would have to set the Sailor free. She swam out to the ocean, found a ship and gently pushed it off course. The Sailor was found and rescued. Before he left he wept and said to the Sea Witch, “Bright Eyes, you’ve been good to me. One day I’ll play my flute again by the sea. I know when I do you’ll come.”

And so it was that the Sailor and the Sea Witch parted. For many years afterwards the Sea Witch roamed the ocean alone, dreaming of her Sailor and his beautiful flute. Sometimes she listened, hoping to find him. Alas, it was no use. She heard no song from the Sailor. Her love had vanished.

©1998 N. Dollak

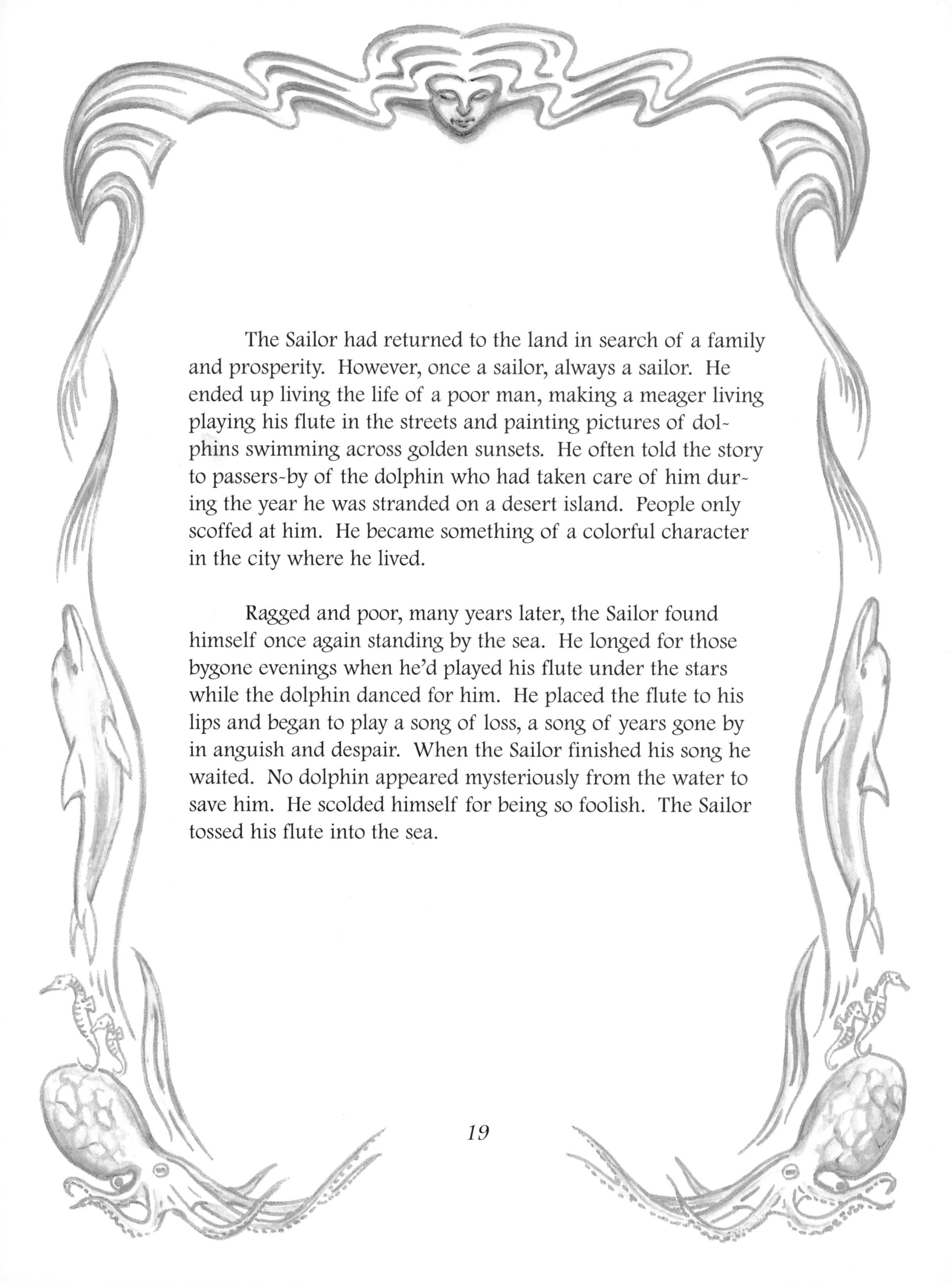

The Sailor had returned to the land in search of a family and prosperity. However, once a sailor, always a sailor. He ended up living the life of a poor man, making a meager living playing his flute in the streets and painting pictures of dolphins swimming across golden sunsets. He often told the story to passers-by of the dolphin who had taken care of him during the year he was stranded on a desert island. People only scoffed at him. He became something of a colorful character in the city where he lived.

Ragged and poor, many years later, the Sailor found himself once again standing by the sea. He longed for those bygone evenings when he'd played his flute under the stars while the dolphin danced for him. He placed the flute to his lips and began to play a song of loss, a song of years gone by in anguish and despair. When the Sailor finished his song he waited. No dolphin appeared mysteriously from the water to save him. He scolded himself for being so foolish. The Sailor tossed his flute into the sea.

The Sea Witch had heard. She couldn't bring herself to come to the Sailor when he was in such a grievous way. Instead she watched from afar. After the Sailor left she took the flute.

The Sea Witch rose from the ocean in the form of a beautiful Caribbean Princess. Then from the sea she fashioned a horse and carriage. In her regal carriage she searched the city streets for her love.

©1998 N. Dollak

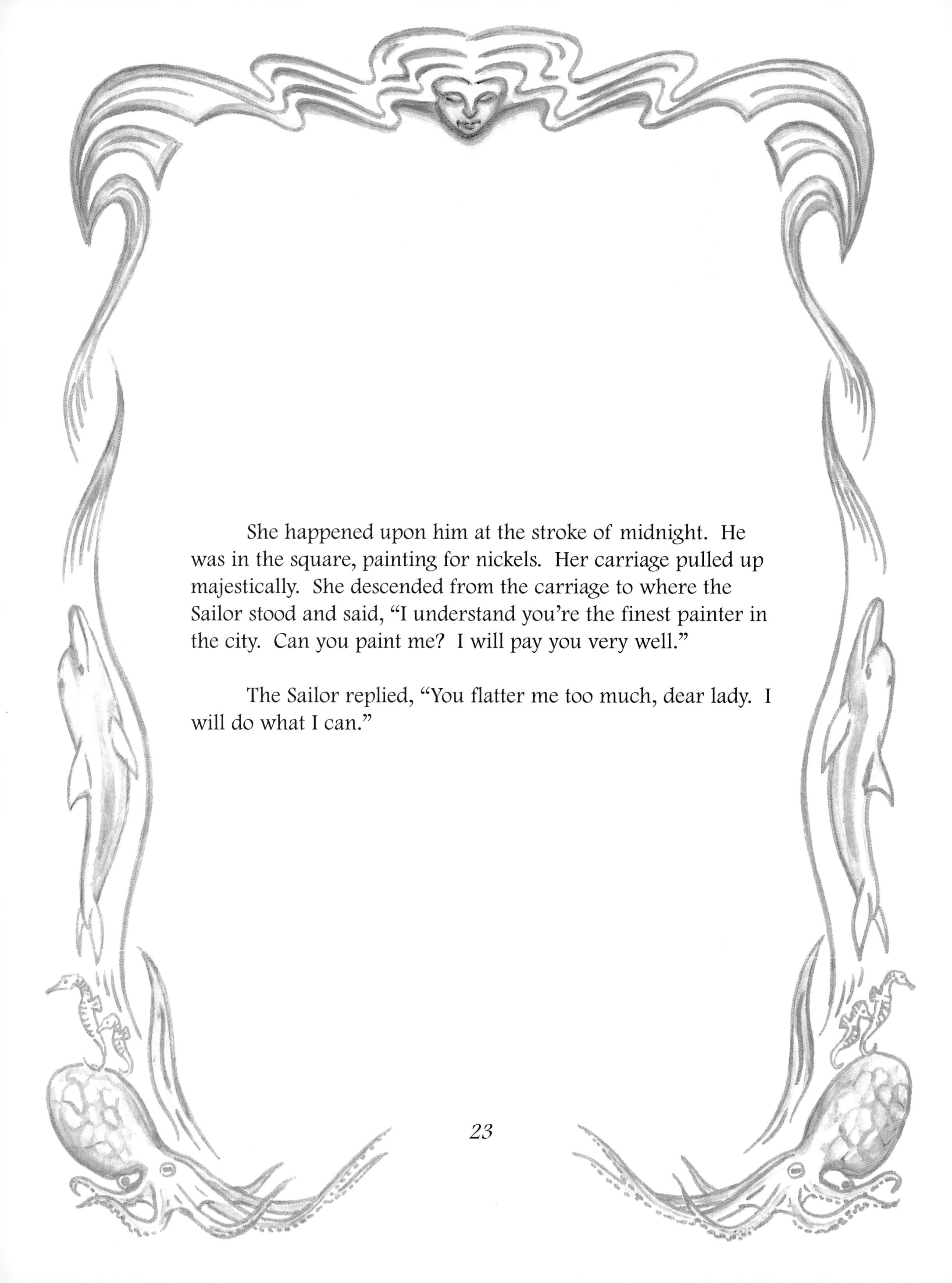

She happened upon him at the stroke of midnight. He was in the square, painting for nickels. Her carriage pulled up majestically. She descended from the carriage to where the Sailor stood and said, “I understand you’re the finest painter in the city. Can you paint me? I will pay you very well.”

The Sailor replied, “You flatter me too much, dear lady. I will do what I can.”

The Sailor set about painting. He found that his hands leapt to life. Painting the mysterious woman was magnificent. It was as if she were an old love who had stirred his heart once more. He molded and shaped every detail of her face with delight. When he came to her eyes he suddenly stopped.

© 1998 N. Dollak

*Her eyes?* he thought to himself. Funny; he hadn't noticed them when she'd stepped out of the carriage. Her eyes were so familiar... like those of the dolphin in the sea so long ago.

The woman became impatient. "Why have you stopped?" she asked.

"Forgive me," the Sailor said. "For a moment I was taken away. You remind me of something. Ah... It was nothing. Just the ramblings of a poor man."

The Sailor continued painting. He thought he detected the slightest trace of a smile across the woman's lips.

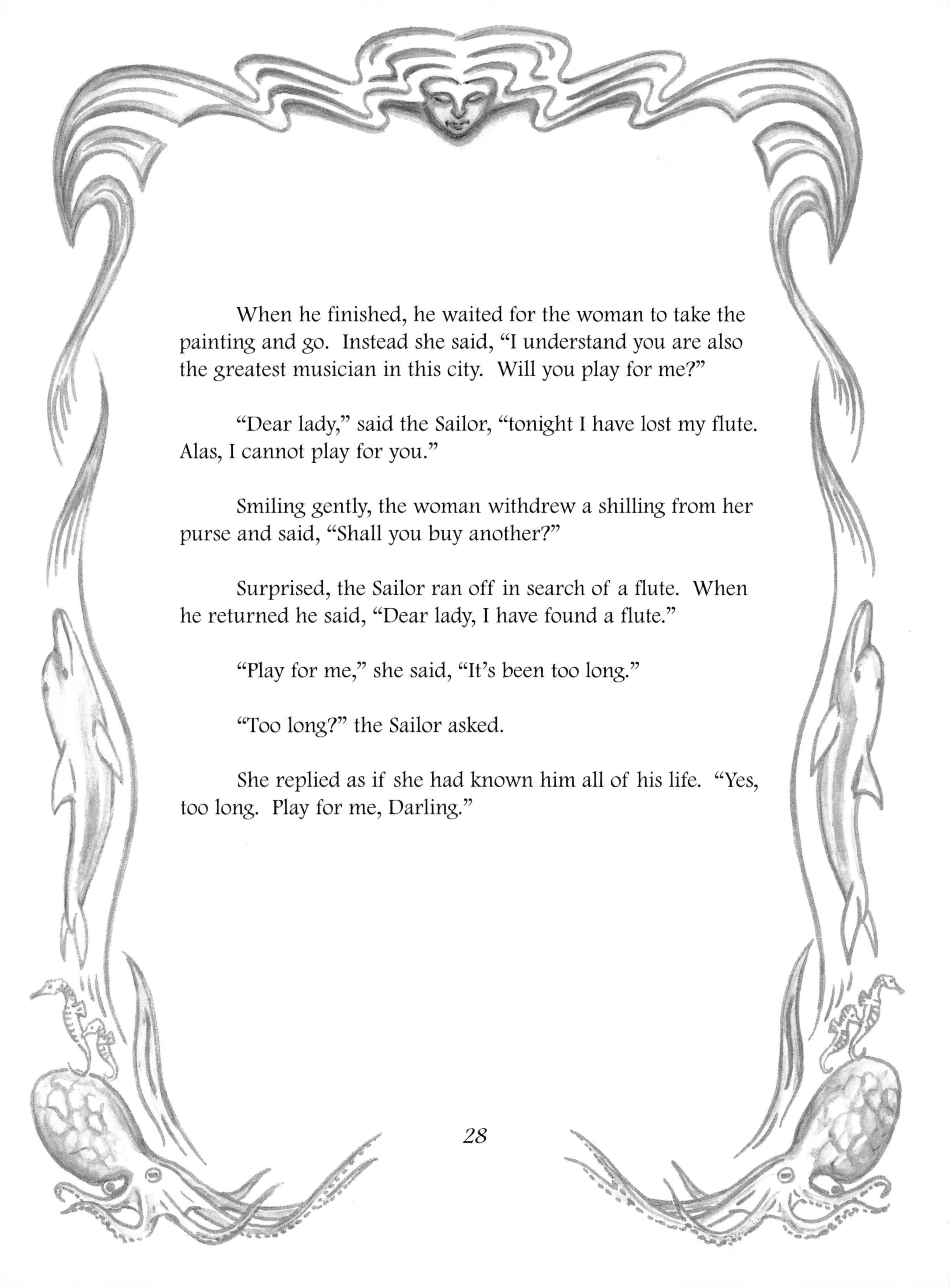

When he finished, he waited for the woman to take the painting and go. Instead she said, “I understand you are also the greatest musician in this city. Will you play for me?”

“Dear lady,” said the Sailor, “tonight I have lost my flute. Alas, I cannot play for you.”

Smiling gently, the woman withdrew a shilling from her purse and said, “Shall you buy another?”

Surprised, the Sailor ran off in search of a flute. When he returned he said, “Dear lady, I have found a flute.”

“Play for me,” she said, “It’s been too long.”

“Too long?” the Sailor asked.

She replied as if she had known him all of his life. “Yes, too long. Play for me, Darling.”

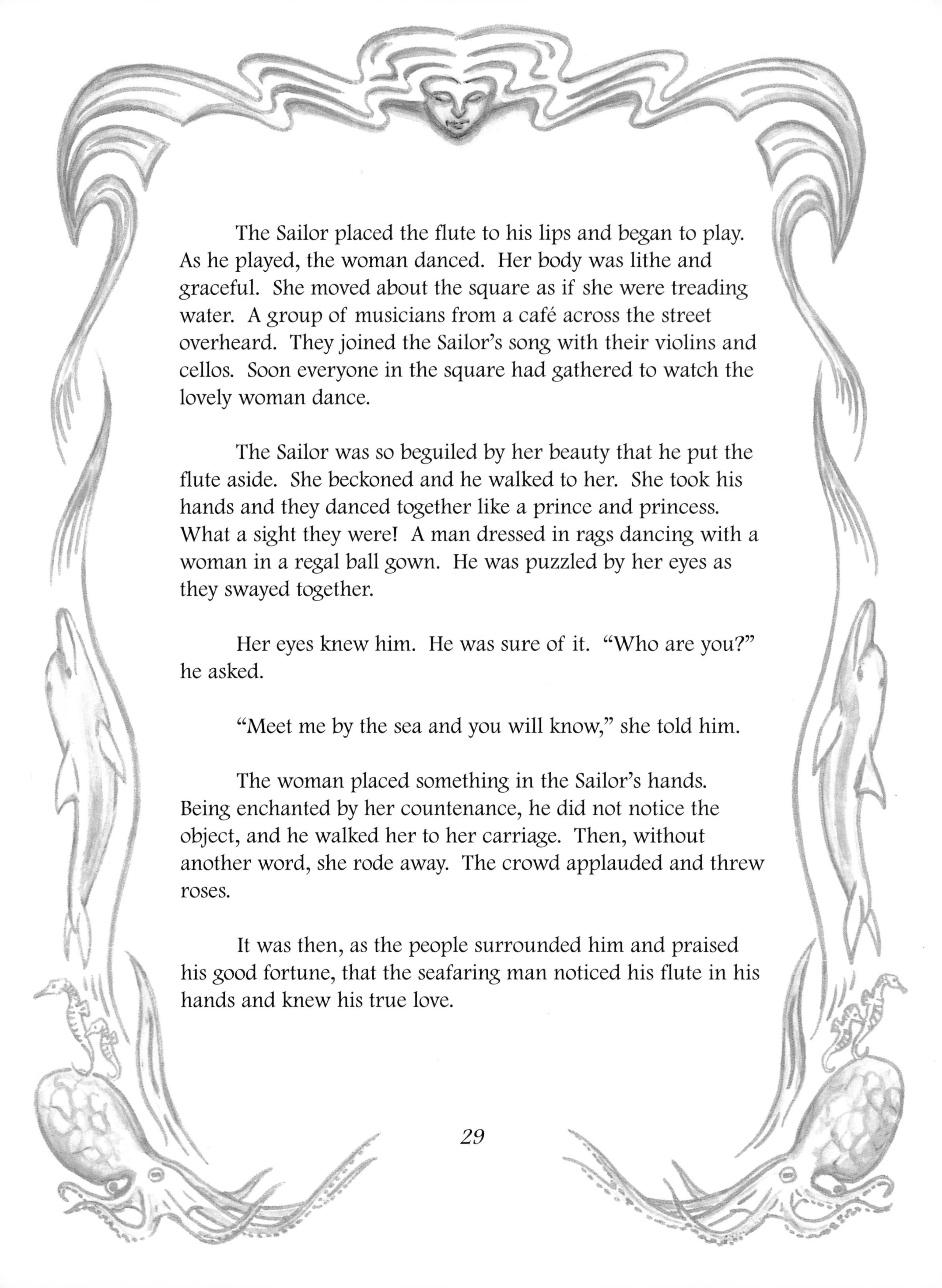

The Sailor placed the flute to his lips and began to play. As he played, the woman danced. Her body was lithe and graceful. She moved about the square as if she were treading water. A group of musicians from a café across the street overheard. They joined the Sailor's song with their violins and cellos. Soon everyone in the square had gathered to watch the lovely woman dance.

The Sailor was so beguiled by her beauty that he put the flute aside. She beckoned and he walked to her. She took his hands and they danced together like a prince and princess. What a sight they were! A man dressed in rags dancing with a woman in a regal ball gown. He was puzzled by her eyes as they swayed together.

Her eyes knew him. He was sure of it. "Who are you?" he asked.

"Meet me by the sea and you will know," she told him.

The woman placed something in the Sailor's hands. Being enchanted by her countenance, he did not notice the object, and he walked her to her carriage. Then, without another word, she rode away. The crowd applauded and threw roses.

It was then, as the people surrounded him and praised his good fortune, that the seafaring man noticed his flute in his hands and knew his true love.

DON'T SIT ON LEDGE
©1998 N. Dollak

He disappeared into the crowd and was never seen in the city again. He went to the beach and found the Sea Witch and her carriage perched above the ocean. The Sailor felt no fear of sinking as he walked across the water to where she waited.

When he kissed his love beneath the moon, the carriage sank into the sea.

Two dolphins rose from the water.

So it was that the Sailor returned to his only love, the sea.

◆ *THE END* ◆

# *HOW WE MAKE A BOOK*

A Malibu Books for Children "Featurette"
by Nicholas Dollak

Have you ever wondered how books get made? I mean, *really* made? Some people might think it's very easy. They might say something like, "Well, the author sits down and writes the story, sends it off to a publisher, and then the publisher prints it as a book. If it's got pictures, an illustrator makes the pictures and they get put into the book."

Well… that's *sort* of how it happens. But it's not *that* easy. Anyone who's ever tried to make a book can tell you that it's a *lot* of work!

When I was very young, I tried my hand at creating books. I would staple several sheets of paper together. Then I would draw the cover art, give the book a title, and proceed to fill it with pictures and text. Sometimes I would run out of pages before I was done; sometimes I would run out of story before I ran out of pages! I never let it bother me, though; if the story wasn't finished, I would attach more paper as needed. And I could usually fill up extra pages with more drawings.

As the years went by, I learned more about how books are made. When I was in eighth grade, I wrote and illustrated an adventure novel called *The Third Ice Age*. Later, when I was in college, I re-did the illustrations and re-wrote the book. After college, I sent it around to publishers, but nobody would publish it. A few of them were curious about the illustrations, though, so I figured I'd impress them by mailing them a bound copy of the book, with the illustrations in place, that looked a lot like something you'd see in bookstores. (When a manuscript is sent to a publisher, it's a stack of loose pages typed on one side only and placed in a flat box, and doesn't resemble a book at all.) So I took a copying machine, scissors and glue, and made a "master copy" of *The Third Ice Age* with all pictures. From this I could make copies that looked sort of like something you see in bookstores. I even printed up front and back covers, mounted them on posterboard, and very carefully spread wet glue over the spine to bind it all together. As a finishing touch, I glued a strip of paper with the title printed on it over the spine, and stuck clear contact paper over the cover to protect it.

Although no publishers accepted my book, I got a lot of compliments on my interesting "sample copy!" I managed to sell a few in small, independently-run bookstores. To make things easier, I designed and built a wooden box in which I could bind two copies at a time.

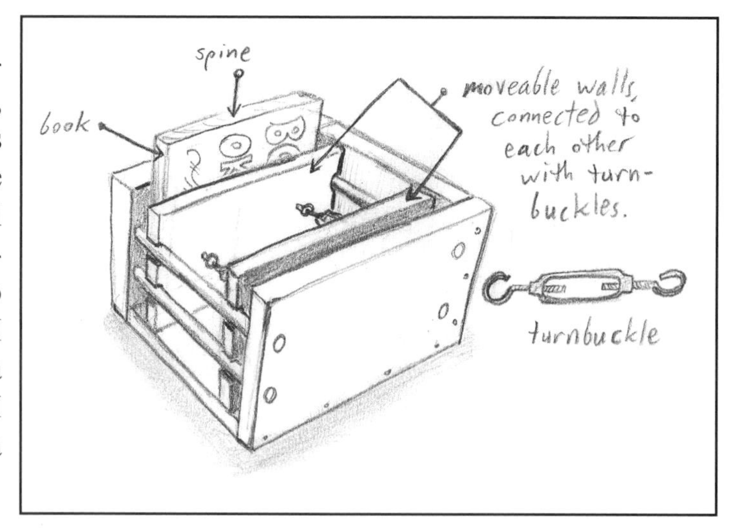


In 1993, Preston McClear, a friend of mine from high school, ran into me and asked if I'd illustrate a children's book he'd written. Of course I said I'd take a crack at it, and before long we were producing little hand-made copies of finished books and selling them in local stores. A guest bedroom at my parents' house became my print-shop, where I would run my photocopiers and bind my books. With Preston's marketing skills, we soon began to get orders for books, and I had to produce batches of ten, twenty or even thirty copies! It got so that my little wooden box was not enough to bind everything in time. For a little while I considered building a couple more --- then I hit upon an ingenious yet simple solution: potato-chip bag clips!

That's right --- those broad little plastic clips, available in fine grocery stores everywhere, were perfect for holding the books together while the glue dried. I now only needed the binder for the part where I applied the glue. After that, I could attach a couple of clips, lift the book out and set it aside to dry.

It was still a lot of work, though. Sometimes I'd be working in that room for hours at a stretch, printing one book while binding another, with stacks of paper all around the room, and a bunch of drying copies standing against the wall with clips sticking up from their spines like stegosaur plates. Even after the glue had dried and the spines had been covered, I still had to stick the clear contact paper on

--- it would take about an hour just to cover ten copies, since there was measuring, cutting, careful peeling and placing, and finally careful trimming involved... not to mention a *huge* clean-up job afterward.

In the meantime, Preston set up a company called Malibu Books For Children and learned a lot about how the publishing business works. Eventually, we decided to get *The Boy Under the Bed* officially printed --- by a real printer. This is very expensive, but in the long run costs less than making the books by hand. Also, the books are much sturdier and look better in many ways.

Even though the printing is now done by someone else, Preston and I still do a lot of the work. I do the page layout on my computer, using a program called Quark XPress, and design the look of the entire book. Why do we do all this? Well, it's cheaper than paying someone else to do it, for one. Also, it gives us total creative control. Remember, I'm an artist. Every detail of this book is important, even the font.

Okay, so... where do the books come from before we get them printed?

It starts when Preston comes up with an idea. He gets most of his ideas when he's taking a bath, or going to work, or brushing his teeth! Then he does what is probably the best thing to do when an idea hits: he writes it down. Later, he looks over the idea and starts writing the actual story, based on the idea. Every so often, he re-reads what he's written and makes changes, polishing his story like a gemstone until it shines the way he wants it to.

Then he gives me a copy and tells me which parts he wants illustrated and how he wants the pictures to look. I sketch out small drawings on scratch paper, which he looks at to make sure we're thinking along the same lines.

Later, I draw the pictures full-size on 11x17-inch Bristol board and show

them to Preston for his approval. Once the details have been settled, I begin painting over the drawings. I use mostly watercolors, especially a kind of watercolor called gouache. It's a little tricky to use, but it can look like oil paints if you know what you're doing. And it

dries much more quickly than oil. Here you can see both the sketch and the finished version of one of the illustrations for *The Sailor and the Sea Witch*.

Meanwhile, Preston re-reads his story and looks for ways to improve it. He'll add a paragraph here, delete a sentence there, change a word in this line or that. Sometimes I catch a spelling error, or find a misused word, and I point it out. And sometimes he catches a mistake in my drawings! It's good to get someone else's input.

Finally, the illustrations are all painted. This can take at least two months, but it depends on how much time I have to work on the pictures, how complex they are, and how many there are. Preston looks them over, I make whatever changes are necessary… and then we're ready to prepare a Quark XPress file for the printer.

When we're done, I copy the file onto a ZIP disk (These files are too large to fit on ordinary disks), and Preston and I send the disk, along with an unbound copy of the book, off to the print shop. We also send the original pictures, which the printer will photograph to make the color separations, which are what print shops use to make really good copies of pictures --- much better than any color copier can do.

The printer has just the right equipment to make books. In a few weeks, Preston and I get a copy of our book, beautifully printed and bound, with a dust jacket. We look it over to make sure it's perfect, and if it is, we thank the printer and ask him or her to make the rest of the books. The print shop sends my illustrations back to me; and in a few months, the copies arrive --- ready to grace fine bookshelves everywhere, including your own.